The
Slumber Party
Secret

Nancy squeezed her eyes shut and asked herself a question: Who stole the party invitations—and why?

Then Nancy opened her eyes. "You know what I think?" she said.

But her friends Bess and George weren't paying any attention to her.

George was watching the video. Bess was staring at something behind Nancy. Before Nancy could turn around, Bess opened her mouth as wide as she could and screamed.

Nancy turned around. Framed in the window was a horrible, scary monster!

THE
NANCY DREW
NOTEBOOKS®

The Slumber Party Secret

CAROLYN KEENE
ILLUSTRATED BY ANTHONY ACCARDO

SCHOLASTIC INC.

New York   Toronto   London   Auckland   Sydney
Mexico City   New Delhi   Hong Kong   Buenos Aires

ISBN 0-439-41979-4

12 11 10 9   8 9 10/0

Printed in the U.S.A.   40

First Scholastic printing, September 2002

The text in this book was set in Excelsior.

1

Party Problems

"But how can party invitations just disappear?" Nancy Drew asked. She stopped right in the middle of the sidewalk and looked at her friend.

"Don't ask me," Rebecca Ramirez moaned. "All I know is my birthday party is ruined. Now no one will come!" She stuck out her lower lip and pouted.

Nancy took Rebecca's hand and started walking down the tree-lined street again to Carl Sandburg Elementary School. They were in third grade there.

Both eight-year-old girls lived just a few blocks from school. This was the first year that Nancy's and Rebecca's parents had let them walk to school. For

1

two weeks now, they had walked together every day.

They lived on different streets. But
every morning Nancy stopped to pick
Rebecca up. They were starting to be
good friends.

"I'll come to your party," Nancy said.
Then she put her hand over her mouth.
"Oops! I mean, *if* I'm invited."

"Of course you are, silly," Rebecca
said. "I'm only allowed to invite eight
people, though, because it's a slumber
party." She told Nancy whom she was
inviting.

"Well, why don't you just *ask* everyone to come?" Nancy said. "Then when
you find the invitations, you can give
them out."

"No, no, no," Rebecca said. "You
don't understand. The invitations aren't
lost. They've been stolen!"

"Stolen?" Nancy said.

Rebecca nodded.

"Okay," Nancy said. "Tell me
everything."

Rebecca sighed dramatically. "I don't
know why I'm even going to school. I

should go back home and spend the rest of my life in bed!"

Nancy brushed her reddish blond bangs out of her eyes and smiled. Rebecca was acting upset. *Acting* was the right word, too. Nancy knew that Rebecca wanted to be an actress when she grew up. She always made a big drama out of everything.

She's probably acting more upset than she really is, Nancy thought. Still, a party was important. Especially a slumber party! This would be Nancy's first one.

"Here's the worst part," Rebecca went on. "I made the invitations myself. It took three hours! I put a party favor in each one. So the favors are gone, too!"

"Maybe that's why someone took the invitations," Nancy said. "For the party favors."

"You could be right," Rebecca said. "They were really pretty, too—hair clips made with lots of tiny rainbow ribbons."

Nancy frowned. "I would love to have a rainbow ribbon hair clip," she said. "Maybe I can help you get them back."

3

"Really?" said Rebecca. She flipped her long black hair over her shoulders. "But how?"

"I'll start by asking you questions," Nancy said. She thought for a minute. "When did the invitations disappear?"

"I don't know," Rebecca said. "I had them yesterday. I don't have time to make more. My party is this Friday night."

"This Friday?" Nancy asked. She was surprised. It was already Wednesday.

Rebecca groaned. "I told you it was a big problem. My mom forgot to mail the invitations. I was going to hand them out in school today."

"Wow. We really have to hurry," Nancy said. "Where were the invitations the last time you saw them?"

"I put them on the kitchen counter by the back door last night," Rebecca said. "Then I went to take a bath."

"Maybe the invitations aren't really stolen," Nancy said. "Maybe you just can't find them. Let's look for them after school."

"I've already looked. Twice!" Rebecca said in a huffy voice.

Nancy grinned. "But I didn't look yet. I'm very good at finding things. I find my dad's keys all the time."

"Okay." Rebecca smiled for the first time that morning. "Maybe you *can* find them. Thanks. You are absolutely my best friend in the whole world, Nancy Drew!"

That wasn't true, and Nancy knew it. Jessie Shapiro was Rebecca's best friend.

Rebecca and Nancy walked into the school building. Then they hurried to their classrooms. Rebecca was in Mrs. Apple's third-grade class. Nancy was in Ms. Spencer's room, at the very end of the hall.

When Nancy got to her classroom, all the other students were in their seats. Nancy closed the classroom door behind her.

"You're almost late!" said George Fayne as Nancy passed her desk at the front of the row.

"I know," said Nancy. The bell rang just as she sat down at her desk by the window.

"Why are you so late?" Bess Marvin asked. Her seat was right next to Nancy's.

"I was talking to Rebecca," Nancy whispered. "I'll tell you at lunch."

Nancy couldn't stop thinking about the missing party invitations. But first she had a different problem to solve: 111 + 32 = ?

For the next hour Ms. Spencer's class did math review. Math was not Nancy's favorite subject. But it was easy for her. Nancy did most of the problems in her head—just to make them harder.

After math the class did science. Then history.

Finally the lunch bell rang.

Nancy and Bess hurried out of the classroom. They met George at the door.

Bess was one of Nancy's two best friends. She was pretty, with long blond hair. Bess was fussy about her hair. She combed it a lot and liked to wear headbands or bows.

George was Bess's cousin. She was Nancy's other best friend. Her real name was Georgia, but no one called her that. She was taller than Nancy and Bess and not fussy about her hair at all. George had dark curls that bounced when she ran. She rarely wore ribbons or headbands. She didn't like anything in her hair that could fall out when she was doing a cartwheel. Or playing hopscotch. Or climbing a tree.

Sometimes the girls brought their lunches. Other times they ate the cafeteria food. That day the three of them went through the lunch line together. Then they found seats at an empty table.

While they ate, Nancy told Bess and George that they were invited to Rebecca's party. Then she told them about the missing party invitations and favors.

George wrinkled her nose. "I don't care about the party favors," she said. "But I can't wait to go to a slumber party! That will be so much fun."

Bess frowned at George. "Well, *I* care about the party favors," Bess said. "I would love to have a rainbow ribbon hair clip."

"Me, too," Nancy agreed. She put a straw into her milk carton. "So I'm going to help Rebecca find the invitations. But I have to work fast. The party is this Friday night."

"This Friday?" Bess said. "Uh-oh."

"Yeah, that's pretty soon," George agreed.

"No, that's not the problem. I think there's going to be trouble at her party," Bess said.

"Why?" Nancy asked.

"Because guess who's having a party the same night? And on the same street where Rebecca lives?"

"Who?" Nancy and George both asked.

Bess pinched her nose closed and scrunched up her face. "The boys!" she said.

2

Hurt Feelings

But that's neat!" Nancy said. She put down her egg salad sandwich. "That makes two slumber parties on Friday. It's like a special sleepover night."

"No, it isn't," Bess said, shaking her head. "The boys will ruin everything!"

"What do you mean?" Nancy asked.

"I heard Jason Hutchings inviting his friends," Bess said. "They're all bringing giant squirt guns. There's going to be a water war."

"Sounds like fun," George said. She popped a pickle into her mouth. "What's wrong with that?"

Bess rolled her eyes. "I told you already! Jason lives down the street from

10

Rebecca. They'll probably all come over and ruin our party."

"How?" George asked.

"Just by being boys!" Bess said. "By acting like jerks!"

"Maybe," Nancy said. "But if they do come, we'll get rid of them. Won't we, George?" Nancy poked George under the table.

"You bet. We'll let them take someone as their prisoner," George continued. "Someone with long blond hair. Someone who—"

"You wouldn't dare!" Bess said.

"Anyway, the boys don't know about Rebecca's party yet," Nancy said. "No one knows except us—because the invitations are missing. And I don't think the boys will care."

"You don't know Jason the way I do," Bess said. "He's such a creep!"

Just then Rebecca came over. "You're all three invited to my party," she announced. "Sorry I don't have invitations. They were stolen by some horrible thief."

"That's all right," Bess said sweetly. "We understand."

"Thanks," Rebecca said. "You guys are my best friends in the whole world!"

The girls looked at one another and tried not to giggle.

"But don't talk about my party in class," Rebecca went on. "It's a secret because my mom said I could only invite eight friends. Okay?"

"Okay," Nancy, Bess, and George said together.

Rebecca started to walk away. "And bring your sleeping bags!" she called back to them in a loud voice. Then she hurried over to another table.

Nancy watched as Rebecca whispered something to Sarah Churnichan and Katie Zaleski. Next Rebecca whispered to Jessie Shapiro, her best friend. Then she walked over to two other third-grade girls. She didn't even bother whispering to them. She invited them to the party out loud.

"Oh, boy," Nancy said. "She tells us to keep the party a secret. Then she blabs it all over the place!"

"Blabs what?" someone behind Nancy asked.

Nancy turned around in her chair. Jason Hutchings was standing right behind her.

"Don't tell him!" Bess cried.

"Don't tell him!" Jason repeated. He made his voice high and imitated Bess. He burped on purpose. Then he laughed loud enough for everyone around to hear and walked away.

"See what I mean?" Bess said. "He's a jerk! He'll ruin Rebecca's party for sure."

"Not if we keep it a secret," Nancy said. She bit into a cookie.

"Keep what a secret?" There was a new voice at Nancy's back.

Nancy turned around. Why was everyone listening to her today?

Now Lindsay Mitchell was standing there, holding an empty lunch bag. Lindsay liked to eavesdrop. She always ended up hearing things she shouldn't have. Then she got her feelings hurt.

"I can't tell you what we were talking about," Nancy said. "I promised I wouldn't."

"I already know," Lindsay said. "It's

about Rebecca's party, isn't it? I can't believe she didn't invite me."

Nancy felt her face turn red. "It's a slumber party, Lindsay. Rebecca's mother said she could only invite a few friends. Rebecca didn't want to hurt anyone's feelings."

"Then she shouldn't have talked about it at school!" Lindsay said.

That was true, and Nancy knew it.

"I'll never invite her to a party as long as I live," Lindsay said. Then she stomped off.

Bess, Nancy, and George picked up their cafeteria trays, emptied them in the trash, and stacked them on the shelf. Then they went outside.

Nancy loved going outside at lunchtime. But the playground wasn't much fun that day. Before lunchtime was over, a lot of the third-grade girls had divided up into two groups.

Rebecca was in the middle of one group, with the eight girls who had been invited to her party. They were playing on the swings.

Lindsay Mitchell was in the middle of

the other group. She was with some of the girls who had not been invited. They weren't playing anything at all. They were just standing around and talking.

When the bell rang, everyone went inside. The boys pushed and shoved. They were trying to get to the water fountain first.

"This is my first slumber party ever," Jessie said as they waited to get a drink.

"Mine, too," Nancy said.

"Can we have a pillow fight?" Jessie asked.

"Sure," said Rebecca.

"*Ooooh*. A pillow fight!" Jason said. "How exciting. NOT!"

Jason and his friends laughed. Mike Minelli laughed so hard he spit water all over the floor.

"Just ignore them," Bess said. She grabbed Nancy's wrist and pulled her into the classroom.

In the afternoon Nancy's class worked on language arts. First they read aloud. Then they wrote out their spelling words. Last they worked on handwriting.

Nancy loved making fancy capital *N*'s and capital *D*'s.

Finally school was over. Nancy quickly stuffed her books in her backpack. Then she went outside. Rebecca was waiting for her by the school's front door.

"Where have you been?" Rebecca asked. "I thought I'd *die* waiting for you!"

"Rebecca, the bell just rang," Nancy said. "You couldn't have been waiting that long."

Then Nancy noticed that Rebecca looked very upset. She wasn't acting. "What's wrong?" Nancy asked.

"Look!" Rebecca said. She shoved a piece of paper at Nancy. "Someone put this horrible note on my desk."

Nancy opened the note. It was printed in big letters, in green ink. There were only seven words on the page. Seven *creepy* words. The message gave Nancy a chill. It said:

"You'll be sorry. Your party is doomed!"

3

Green Ink
and Garbage Cans

It *is* horrible," Nancy said to Rebecca. She stared at the note. "Who wrote it?"

"It was on my desk when I came in after lunch," Rebecca said. "Anyone could have put it there."

Lindsay Mitchell was the first person Nancy thought of. Nancy remembered how angry Lindsay had been at lunch. Also, Lindsay was in Rebecca's class. But Nancy knew that someone from her own class could have written the note, too.

Nancy looked at the note again. It was on the kind of lined paper that everyone used in third grade.

"Someone is really trying to wreck my party," Rebecca complained. "First the invitations. Now this!"

"Let's go to your house. It's time to see if the invitations really have disappeared," Nancy said. "I'll have to call home, though, so our housekeeper knows where I am."

Rebecca's face brightened. "You really *are* going to help me, aren't you?" She sounded surprised.

"I promised, didn't I?" Nancy said. "Of course I'll help." Why wouldn't she? This was fun! It was just like being a detective.

"Thanks," Rebecca said. For once Nancy knew she really meant it.

"Can I keep the note?" Nancy asked. "Maybe I can find out if someone in my class prints like this. Then you can try to find out if anyone in your class prints like this. Okay?"

"Okay," Rebecca said.

The two girls walked to Rebecca's house. Mrs. Ramirez said hello to Nancy and showed her where the phone was. She made them a snack of peanut butter crackers and apple juice. Then she went to the family room, in the basement. The girls ate at the big oval counter in the kitchen.

Nancy tried to think where the party invitations could be. She picked up a cracker and walked around.

She looked in the oven, the freezer, the cookie jar, and the broom closet. She looked in every kitchen cabinet and drawer. Then she scratched her head.

"Is this where you put them last night?" Nancy asked. She pointed to the counter where Rebecca was still eating her snack.

"Nmmph. Thaa wrrd gnmnep bikdr," Rebecca said. Her mouth was full of crackers.

Nancy giggled. So did Rebecca. Tiny cracker crumbs sprayed out of her mouth. That made Nancy really laugh. Rebecca laughed even more.

Finally they stopped laughing. Rebecca took a big gulp of apple juice. So did Nancy.

"Now tell me again," Nancy said. "Where did you leave the invitations?"

"On the counter by the kitchen door," Rebecca said. "That's where I put things so I'll remember to take them to school in the morning."

Nancy looked at the other counter. It was just an ordinary counter. No holes for the invitations to fall into. No wastebasket nearby. No piles of junk mail or magazines for the invitations to get lost in.

Where could they have gone?

"Did you ask your brother? Or your parents?" Nancy asked. "Maybe someone mailed them after all."

Rebecca shook her head. "I asked my dad and mom. They said no. Stupid Todd said I probably threw them away by accident." Rebecca frowned. "You're lucky you don't have a big brother."

Nancy knew that Rebecca's twelve-year-old brother teased her a lot. But he might be right, Nancy thought. Sometimes people threw important things away without thinking.

"Why don't we look in the garbage just to be sure," Nancy said.

Rebecca sighed and got down from

her stool. "Okay. But I don't think we'll find them. Come on."

Nancy followed Rebecca out the kitchen door. "The garbage can is next to the garage," Rebecca said, pointing. "You look—I'll wait here."

Nancy walked over to the garbage can. She lifted the lid and looked inside.

Yuck! She couldn't look through all those bags. And Rebecca's mom would have a fit if they dumped them out.

"Hey! Why are you snooping in someone else's garbage?" called a voice behind Nancy.

Nancy whirled around and saw Laura McCorry. Laura was in Rebecca's class. She lived across the street from Rebecca. Nancy remembered that Laura and Rebecca used to play together. They didn't seem to be friends anymore, though.

"You scared me," Nancy said. "And you're the third person who's snuck up on me today."

"I'm not sneaking up," Laura said. "I came to see Rebecca. What are you looking for, anyway?"

"Uh, I was looking for something that

Rebecca lost," Nancy said. She didn't want to say anything about the party. She knew Laura wasn't invited.

"What?"

"My homework," Rebecca answered, walking up to them. She gave Nancy a look that said Don't tell Laura about the party.

"Your homework?" Laura asked.

"I think I threw it in the trash by mistake," Rebecca lied.

Laura leaned forward and looked into the garbage can. "Well, I wouldn't go in there to look for it if I were you," she said.

"I guess I'll have to do it all over again." Rebecca shrugged. "Oh, well."

"Can I come in?" Laura said. "I wanted to ask if I could borrow your tape player."

"Sure," Rebecca said. Nancy could tell Rebecca was in a hurry to get away from the garbage. Nancy was, too. It really did smell awful!

When they got inside, Rebecca ran up to her room. A minute later she came back with a small tape player. She gave it to Laura.

When Laura was gone, Rebecca wrinkled her nose and made a face. "I don't really like her," Rebecca told Nancy. "But her mom and my mom are best friends, so I have to be nice to her." Then she added, "It's good that her mother drives her to school on her way to work. That way she doesn't have to walk with us."

Nancy liked Laura and wouldn't have minded if they walked to school together. "Do you think she knows about your party?" Nancy asked.

"I don't know. Why?"

"Because I think her feelings might be hurt if she did know," Nancy said. "Really, I think a lot of the girls felt left out."

"Like who?" Rebecca put her hands on her hips.

"Like Lindsay Mitchell," Nancy said. "She was upset at lunch."

Rebecca let her hands drop. "I knew that would happen," she said. "I saw Lindsay in the playground. Boy, did she look mad. Do you think she sent me the note?"

"I don't know," Nancy said. That was a

hard question to answer. Nancy couldn't tell much from the printing. Maybe it was from a girl. Maybe it was from a boy.

Nancy looked at her watch. "I have to go home now. Maybe we can work on this some more tomorrow."

"We have to," Rebecca said. "My party is only two days away."

"I know," Nancy said. "And before the party, I want to find out who wrote that creepy note."

"Me, too," Rebecca said. "And then I'll never speak to them again!" She flipped her hair over her shoulders with both hands when she said that.

Rebecca looked so silly that Nancy had to laugh. "See you tomorrow," she called as she went out the back door.

Nancy thought about the party all the way home. Her best friends would be there. Maybe they would stay up late and tell stories. And have a pillow fight. And eat popcorn. Being old enough to sleep over was exciting!

Except for one thing. What if the note was true? What if Rebecca's party really was doomed?

4

Nancy's New Notebook

Hannah! Guess what? Rebecca Ramirez invited me to her slumber party on Friday night!" Nancy said as she rushed through the back door of her house.

Hannah Gruen was standing at the sink, peeling carrots. She was the family housekeeper. She had been living with the Drews ever since Nancy was three years old. That was when Nancy's mother had died. Hannah was middle-aged, with graying hair and a sweet face. She was like a mother to Nancy.

"That's exciting!" Hannah said. "But you've never been to a slumber party before. You'll have to ask your father if it's okay."

For a moment Nancy looked worried. "You don't think he'll say no, do you?"

Hannah laughed. "Your father never can say no to you. I'm sure he'll let you go."

She handed Nancy a carrot. "How was school?"

"It was okay," Nancy said. "Too much math review. I wish we'd start learning something new."

Hannah laughed again. "You *always* want to learn something new," she said.

Nancy took a bite of carrot and looked at the clock on the wall. "When Dad gets home, I want to ask him about the party. And maybe we could go shopping for Rebecca's present right after dinner. The party's only two days away!"

"You're in luck," Hannah said. "Your father's home early today."

When Nancy heard that, her whole face lit up. Her dad was home? That was great!

Carson Drew was a lawyer. He knew all about mysteries and crimes. He was always solving problems for other people. Maybe he could help with Rebecca's party problem.

Nancy ran through the big old house until she reached the staircase. Then she hurried up the carpeted steps and into her room to put her school things away.

She hurried downstairs again and knocked on the door to her father's study. It was the rule. Always knock before entering.

"Come in," Carson Drew called out.

Nancy burst in the door of the wood-paneled room. "Hi, Daddy!"

"Hi there, Pudding Pie," he said with a smile.

Nancy smiled back. Pudding Pie was his special name for her. He had called her that ever since she was four years old. That's when Nancy had tried to eat a huge piece of chocolate pudding pie with her hands. She had gotten chocolate all over her face! It was even in her hair. Her father had taken a picture of her looking like that. It was in one of their photo albums.

"Guess what, Daddy?" Nancy said.

But before he could guess, she told him about the slumber party. "May I go, Daddy? May I?"

"You want to go to a party to *sleep*?" Carson Drew asked. "Sounds pretty boring to me. In fact, it puts me to sleep just thinking about it." He closed his eyes and pretended to snore.

"Daaddy!" Nancy said. "Stop teasing."

Carson Drew opened his eyes and laughed. "Of course you can go, Pudding Pie."

Nancy gave her father a big hug. "Thanks, Daddy." Then she told him about the missing invitations. And about the note written in green ink.

"Hmmm," said Carson Drew. He leaned back in his big leather chair. "Sounds like a mystery."

"It is!" Nancy said. "I've been trying to figure out if the invitations were really stolen. And who wrote the note. Can you help?"

Carson Drew got a twinkle in his eye. "I sure can," he said.

He opened one of the drawers in his large oak desk and reached inside. He pulled out a small notebook with a shiny blue cover.

"It sounds as if you're turning into a detective," he said. "So I'm giving you this special notebook. Use it to write down anything that seems like a clue. I'll bet you'll figure out the mystery faster that way."

A new notebook? Nancy smiled. She loved notebooks! And this one was especially nice. It had a pocket inside, and blue was her favorite color.

"Thanks," she said. "Oh, and Daddy, can we go shopping tonight? I need to get a birthday present for Rebecca. The party is on Friday."

"I don't see why not," Carson said with a smile.

Nancy gave him another hug. Then she ran out of the study. She hurried up the stairs to her room.

Maybe I *can* be a detective! Nancy thought. That would be fun. Besides, Rebecca needed help. Her party was only two days away.

Nancy sat down at her desk. She opened the notebook. The first page was fresh and clean. She took out her favorite pen from her book bag. She was careful to use her best handwriting.

At the top of the page she wrote:

Rebecca's Party Invitations

Then she wrote:

On counter by back door Tuesday night. Gone Wednesday morning.

Who is coming?
Me, Bess, George, Jessie Shapiro, Katie Zaleski, Sarah Churnichan, Courtney Nilsson, Amara Shane.

Note to Rebecca. Green ink: "You'll be sorry. Your party is doomed!"

She also wrote:

Jason's party—same night!

Then Nancy put the notebook in her backpack so she would have it with her every day at school.

After dinner that night Carson Drew took Nancy to the toy store. Bess and George came along, too. That way they could all get presents for Rebecca.

At the toy store Nancy picked out a very special music box with butterfly pictures on it. Bess bought Rebecca a unicorn stationery kit. It had paper, envelopes, and stickers. George decided to give her a funny stuffed troll with purple teeth.

After that Nancy, Bess, and George looked at all the stuffed animals.

"I wish it was my birthday," Bess said.

"I know what you mean," Nancy admitted. "It's hard to shop for someone else, especially in a toy store."

The three girls were about to go find Carson Drew, when Bess grabbed Nancy's arm. "Hey, look who's in the sports aisle," Bess whispered to Nancy.

"Who?"

"David Berger and Mike Minelli." Nancy knew they were two of Jason's best friends.

"Do you think they saw us?" Bess whispered. "And what are they doing here tonight, anyway?"

"I'll bet they're buying birthday presents for Jason," Nancy said.

"Yuck!" Bess said. "Let's go!"

"No, wait," Nancy said. She went up to David Berger.

"Hi," Nancy said.

"Hi," David said without looking at her. He was dribbling a basketball.

"You're in Rebecca Ramirez's class, aren't you?" Nancy said.

"So?"

"I wondered if you saw anyone put a note on her desk today?" Nancy asked.

"Huh?" David said. He looked up.

"A note written in green ink," said Nancy.

David shrugged. "I don't know." He passed the ball to Mike, who pretended to shoot. Nancy got angry. They were acting as if she weren't even there.

Nancy went back to Bess and George. "They say they don't know anything," she said. "But I don't believe them."

"Me, either," Bess said. "Look."

Nancy turned around and saw Mike and David watching her. Then they started whispering. Mike put his hand over his mouth to hide what he was saying. Then they both burst out laughing and stomped their feet. They gave each other high fives.

"Have a good party," Mike yelled to the girls. "If you can!"

5
Another Note

Nancy got up early Thursday morning. She got dressed and then sat at her desk. All night she had been thinking of a plan. Now she was ready.

She took out a blank piece of paper. At the top, she wrote "IMPORTANT" in big letters.

Then Nancy wrote:

We are the students of Ms. Spencer's third-grade class. We would like Ms. Spencer to think about doing these things:

- Give us two hours of free time each week to do anything we want.

- Let us have a puppy in the class-room instead of just a pet in a cage.
- Let us read comic books for at least one of our weekly reading reports.

Then Nancy drew twenty-five blank lines at the bottom of the page. One space for each person in her class to sign.

Then she made another copy. It was exactly the same except that Mrs. Apple's name was on it.

On the way to school she told Rebecca about her plan. They ran into Bess and George in the school hallway. Nancy showed them the two papers.

"Are you nuts?" Bess said. "The teachers will never let us do this stuff."

"I know," Nancy said. She gave Bess a huge grin. "I just want to get everyone to sign. That way I'll see if anyone's printing matches the note that Rebecca got."

"And to see if anyone writes with green ink," Rebecca added.

"Pretty sneaky," Bess said. She flashed Nancy a smile that said I'm glad my best friend is so super smart!

"But what if some people write their names in cursive," George asked, "instead of printing them?"

"I thought of that," Nancy said. "I don't know about Rebecca's class. But only one person in our class uses cursive. Phoebe Archer. Her mother taught her last year. Anyway, it's worth a try. Rebecca's going to do the list for her class. We're going to do it at lunch."

"I'll help," Bess said.

"So will I," George said. "We'll get everyone to sign."

Nancy, Bess, and George got twenty kids' names during lunch and recess. Jessie Shapiro was absent, and Jason had a dentist appointment.

Rebecca got twenty-three names. Amara Shane was absent.

Nancy looked at both lists. All the names were printed except Phoebe's. None of them looked like the printing on the note. And no one had used green ink.

Nancy was disappointed. But she wasn't going to give up.

"I have another idea," Nancy said. "I'm going to check our room before class starts." She turned and raced back into the school.

Students weren't allowed to be in the classrooms during lunch hour. Quietly Nancy sneaked into her room. She didn't touch anything. But she looked at everything lying on top of the desks. No one seemed to have a green pen.

She was just walking out of the classroom when she ran right into her teacher!

"Nancy," Ms. Spencer said. "Were you looking for me?"

"Ummm . . ." Nancy said.

"Someone told me that you have a petition to give me," Ms. Spencer said.

Nancy blushed. "Oh, uh, well, not really. I mean, it's sort of a joke," Nancy said. She held the papers behind her back.

Ms. Spencer held out her hand. "May I see for myself, please?"

Nancy watched her teacher's face as

she read the petition. At first Ms. Spencer frowned, but she kept reading. Then she pressed her lips together. Nancy couldn't tell if she was angry or going to laugh.

Finally Ms. Spencer looked at Nancy. "I'm afraid these things aren't possible," she said. "I love dogs, too. I can understand why you'd want one for the classroom."

Ms. Spencer handed the papers back to Nancy. She gave her a big grin. "You have quite an imagination, Nancy Drew," she added.

Just then the bell rang. Recess was over. Nancy sat down at her desk. Even if she didn't have any answers yet, she was having fun. She felt just like a detective!

By bedtime that night Nancy still had nothing new to write in her notebook. She took it out of her backpack, anyway. She sat cross-legged on her bed. Then she opened the notebook and wrote:

Thursday. 20 signatures in Ms. Spencer's class.

23 signatures in Mrs. Apple's class.
No new clues.

On Friday Nancy and Rebecca walked to school together. It was Rebecca's birthday and the day of the party. Rebecca carried a big box of cupcakes. There was one for each person in her class.

Nancy looked over at the box. "I wish I were in your class," she said.

Rebecca giggled. "Don't worry. We'll have cake at the party tonight. I'll make sure you get a piece with a big icing rose."

Nancy held the school door open for Rebecca. She walked her friend to her cubby. Every third-grader had a cubby. They were in the hallway. Each student's name was printed on colored paper and taped to the top of the cubby.

Nancy helped Rebecca put the box of cupcakes in her cubby.

"See you later," Nancy said. Then she went down the hall to her own classroom. Ms. Spencer was late, and the door was still locked. All the kids were standing around in the hall.

"Rebecca brought cupcakes for her birthday," Nancy told Bess and George.

"Cupcakes? Where?" Jason Hutchings said.

"In Rebecca's cubby," Nancy answered without thinking.

Just then Ms. Spencer arrived. She unlocked the door. Everyone went in and sat down. Ms. Spencer began to call the roll. She called Jason's name, but there was no answer.

Nancy looked at Bess. "Uh-oh," Nancy said.

"Yeah," Bess said. "Major uh-oh."

Ms. Spencer finished calling the roll. A second later Jason raced into the room.

"Here I am!" he called out to Ms. Spencer.

Jason licked his fingers. Nancy saw pink icing at the corners of his mouth.

"Where have you been, Jason?" Ms. Spencer asked.

"I thought you were lost, Ms. Spencer," Jason said. "I was out looking for you."

Everyone laughed, including Nancy.

Ms. Spencer shook her head and smiled, too. Jason was like that, Nancy thought. He could make grown-ups laugh. And he could make them believe almost anything.

"All right, class," Ms. Spencer said. "Take out your math books. It's time for math review."

Nancy rolled her eyes. Not again!

She took out her math book. She also took out her new blue notebook. Quickly she wrote down: "Jason. Stolen cupcake." Maybe it was a clue!

At lunch Rebecca found Nancy.

"I'm going to die," Rebecca said, grabbing Nancy by the wrist. "Wait till you hear what happened!"

"Let me guess," Nancy said. She pretended to think very hard. "I know! Someone stole one of your cupcakes."

"How did you guess?" Rebecca said. Her mouth dropped open in surprise.

Nancy smiled. "Because I know who did it."

"Who?"

"Jason Hutchings," Nancy said. "He

was licking pink icing from his mouth this morning. It's my fault, too. I told him you brought cupcakes."

"It's not your fault," Rebecca said. "It's *his* fault. He gets away with everything! And guess what happened then?"

"What?"

"Well, there weren't enough cupcakes for everyone. And Lindsay Mitchell didn't get one."

"Uh-oh. Bad news," Nancy said.

"Right." Rebecca rolled her eyes. "She has a *big* sweet tooth. She got really mad, too. But that's not all."

"What do you mean?"

Rebecca handed Nancy another note. Like the first one, it was written in green ink. It said, "We have a secret." *Secret* was printed in extra large letters all the way across the page.

"Weird," Nancy said. "When did you get it?"

"I found it in the box of cupcakes," Rebecca said.

"Do you think it was—"

"Jason!" both girls said at once.

Still, Nancy didn't feel sure. "He did

steal the cupcake. He could have put the note in the box then. But what's the secret?"

"I don't know," Rebecca said.

"And why would Jason have sent you that first note saying your party is doomed?"

"I don't know," Rebecca said.

"And how could he have stolen your party invitations?"

"I don't know," Rebecca said.

"Me, either," Nancy said. "But I'm going to find out!"

6

Party Pranks

Hurry, Daddy, we're going to be late for the party!" Nancy said.

She was wearing her favorite long-sleeved flowered dress. Hannah had brushed Nancy's hair until it shone. She stood in the driveway with her arms full. Sleeping bag. Backpack. Rebecca's birthday present and a card.

Nancy had made the birthday card herself with colored markers. On the front she had drawn a big gold star around Rebecca's name. Inside, Nancy wrote, "You're the Star of Your Own Birthday!"

Carson Drew came down the driveway and frowned at Nancy. But she could tell it was only a pretend frown. "What's the rush?" he said. "Why are you in such a hurry to leave home?"

Nancy giggled. "It's just one night, Daddy," she said. "Come on!"

"Yes, yes, I know." He tried to sound serious. "I'm not sure I want you to go. What if I need you for something tonight?"

Nancy laughed again. She knew her father was teasing. "You won't need me, Daddy. It's just one night. Please! I'm going to drop everything!"

"Okay," her father said with a smile. "Let's load up the trunk."

Nancy put her sleeping bag, backpack, and the present in the trunk. Her father drove to Bess's house.

They had to wait because Bess was still getting dressed. Finally she came outside. She was wearing a purple-checked jumper, purple tights, and a purple shirt. Mr. Drew piled Bess's things into the trunk.

Then they picked up George. She was wearing a dress with three big buttons down the front. Mr. Drew put her things into the trunk, too.

"It's a good thing we aren't picking up anyone else," Mr. Drew said. "This trunk won't hold any more sleepover supplies!"

At five o'clock the three friends arrived at Rebecca's party. Mr. Drew helped them take their things into the house. Then he gave Nancy a goodbye kiss and hug.

Mrs. Ramirez took George, Bess, and Nancy out to the backyard. All the other girls were already there. They were playing games.

Rebecca ran up to greet her guests.

"Guess what?" she said, taking Nancy's hand.

"Happy birthday," Nancy said. "What?"

"I got another note! About an hour ago someone rang the doorbell. When I opened the door, no one was there. This note was lying on the doormat."

She handed a piece of paper to Nancy. It said: "We're having a party—and YOU can't come!"

The printing was the same. But this note was written in blue ink.

"I know who sent it," Bess said. "Jason. He lives so close."

"That's what I think, too," Rebecca said. "But he's so dumb. Why does he think I'd want to go to his stupid party, anyway?"

Nancy just looked at the piece of paper. She didn't say a word. It didn't make sense for Jason to have written the note.

Nancy, Bess, and George joined the other girls. But Nancy couldn't forget about the three notes. What did they mean? Had Jason sent them? And if so, what was he planning to do?

She thought about it while they played badminton. She thought about it while they jumped rope.

But she forgot about it when someone felt a drop of rain.

"Let's go in," Katie Zaleski said. "I don't want to get wet."

"No, wait," Rebecca said. "We haven't gone on the treasure hunt yet."

Rebecca's mother had planned a treasure hunt. She came outside and gave each girl a map of the backyard.

"Is it buried treasure?" Nancy asked.

Mrs. Ramirez smiled. "No, it's not buried."

"But is it bigger than a TV?" Nancy asked. "Or is it small enough to fit in a backpack?"

Mrs. Ramirez laughed. "You ask too many questions, Nancy."

"No, she doesn't," Rebecca said. "She asks just the right amount."

Rebecca squeezed Nancy's hand. "Come on. Let's make up teams," she said. "Nancy, George, Sarah, and Jessie can be on my team. Courtney, Bess, Katie, and Amara will be on the other team."

"That's not fair," Bess said. "I'll never find the treasure without Nancy. She's good at finding things. I don't know where to look."

"Just follow the map," Mrs. Ramirez said. "The treasure is hidden near one of the pictures."

Soon the girls were running all over the backyard. The maps were hard to figure out. They didn't have any words on them—just pictures.

One picture was of a peach. Rebecca got that one. It was the peach tree in the corner of the yard. George climbed the tree to see if the treasure was up there. It wasn't.

"I felt rain!" Amara called.

"Who cares?" George called down. "Just keep looking."

There was a picture of a dog on the map. Jessie guessed that it stood for the doghouse. George crawled into the doghouse to see if the treasure was there. It wasn't.

"Did you feel that? It's raining," Katie called from the other side of the yard.

"I didn't feel anything," Nancy said. She looked up at the sky. The sun was shining. How could there be rain? Nancy kept looking for the treasure.

There was a picture of ants. Nancy thought for a while. "I know!" she said. "Ants would be near the picnic table!"

George crawled underneath the table and looked up. "Here it is!" she cried.

Nancy got on her hands and knees so she could see under the table, too. The treasure was in an envelope, taped under the picnic table top.

George pulled it loose and opened it. Inside were nine fancy pencils with fuzzy animal heads on top. They were party favors. Rebecca handed them out.

"Thanks!" Courtney said. She held her fuzzy teddy bear pencil up to her cheek.

Several drops of water fell on Bess's head. One ran down into her eye. "Let's go in," Bess said. "I don't want my kitten pencil to get wet."

Suddenly Nancy felt lots of drops. But the sun was still shining. How strange, she thought.

"Okay, let's go eat pizza and then birthday cake," Rebecca said.

Everyone ran to the deck on the side of Rebecca's house. There was another big picnic table there. It was covered with a pink-and-white paper tablecloth. Pink paper plates and napkins were set at each place.

"Oh, no!" Rebecca cried. She was the first one up the steps to the deck. "No!" she cried again.

Big tears filled Rebecca's eyes. "I hate this birthday! I hate it!" she cried.

Nancy hurried to see what was wrong. She looked at the deck. It was dry. She looked at the tablecloth. It was dry.

She looked at the plates and napkins. They were dry.

Then Nancy looked at the cake. It was decorated with roses and white icing. Mrs. Ramirez hadn't put the candles on it yet, though. Nancy knew that Rebecca had wanted everyone to see the cake first because it was so pretty.

There was one problem.

Someone had stolen the biggest rose from the center of the cake. Now there was a huge, ugly hole on top!

7

Noises in the Night

Jason Hutchings did this, I know he did," Rebecca said. She rubbed her tears away with her hands. Then she stomped into the house. Nancy followed her.

"Mom? Jason's trying to ruin my party!" Rebecca yelled.

"Calm down," Mrs. Ramirez said. She was standing at a kitchen counter, opening boxes of pizza. Rebecca told her about the cake.

"Why don't you and Nancy and your friends eat the pizza at the dining room table? I'll see if I can fix the cake."

"But aren't you going to call Jason's mother?" Rebecca whined. "I know he stole that rose."

"Not right now," her mother said.

Rebecca's mother moved the cake indoors. She put the pink tablecloth and the plates on the dining room table. Everyone was hungry. Nancy ate two slices of pizza with pepperoni.

While they ate, the girls talked about the cake. Who would do such a terrible thing?

"Bess is right. It must be the boys," Courtney said.

"Jason gets away with everything. Everyone knows that," said Sarah.

The other girls agreed. Nancy looked and listened. She was thinking about someone else. Someone with a sweet tooth. Someone who always got her feelings hurt. Someone named Lindsay Mitchell.

There was only one problem. How could Lindsay steal the rose? She didn't even live nearby.

The girls finished eating. Then Rebecca sat at the table and opened her presents. She loved them all. But she especially loved the card Nancy made for her. She cut out the star with her name on it so she could put it on her bed-room door.

"Time for cake!" Rebecca's mother called as she carried it into the room. She had moved the icing roses around to cover the hole. She had also put colored sprin-kles on top. That way the messed-up icing didn't show. With the candles lit, the cake looked perfect, Nancy thought.

Everyone sang "Happy Birthday" to Rebecca. Then she made a wish and blew out the candles.

After cake and ice cream the girls spread out their sleeping bags on the living room floor. It was almost dark outside.

"Time for a scary movie," Rebecca said. She put a video into the tape machine.

"I'm scared just thinking about it," Bess said. She shivered with excitement. "Do we have to watch this?"

"Yes," Rebecca said. "And you have to scream. That's what makes it fun."

Bess looked over toward the front window. She screamed at the top of her lungs.

"Not yet, silly," Rebecca said.

Bess screamed again.

"What's wrong, Bess?" Nancy asked.

Rebecca's mother came running into the room. "What happened?" she asked.

"I saw a shadow through the window. And I heard a noise outside," Bess answered. "I got scared."

Nancy ran to the window to look. Mrs. Ramirez looked out, too.

"There's nothing there," Mrs. Ramirez said. "Maybe you girls shouldn't watch this movie. How about something else?"

"No!" Rebecca said.

"We want to see the movie!" Jessie and Katie cried.

"Okay," Mrs. Ramirez said. "But maybe Bess doesn't want to watch."

"That's okay," Bess said. "I'll watch the movie."

Bess wrapped her sleeping bag around her knees. Nancy sat on the floor, leaning against the couch. The movie started. It was about a haunted house.

Suddenly Bess poked Nancy. "Listen!" Bess whispered. "Did you hear that?"

Nancy nodded. She had heard the noise. So had Jessie. It sounded like something hitting the window.

Jessie jumped up and pressed the Stop button on the VCR.

There it was again! Nancy thought. Everyone heard it this time. Something was moving around in the bushes outside!

Nancy went to the window and looked out.

She couldn't see anyone in the front yard. But across the street she saw a pizza delivery car. The driver was carrying three large pizza boxes to the house.

"Nobody's out there except for a pizza guy. He's taking three pizzas to Laura McCorry's house," Nancy said.

"Are you *sure* no one else is there?" Rebecca asked. She had gotten up and come to the window beside Nancy.

"Pretty sure," Nancy said. "Maybe it was the wind."

"Then let's watch the movie," Katie said.

"Go ahead," Nancy said. "I'll be right back. I want to get something first."

Nancy went to her backpack and took out her new blue notebook and a pen. Then she curled up on the floor beside Bess. Nancy opened the notebook to a blank page and started to write. But her pen was out of ink.

"Does anyone have a pen I can borrow?" Nancy asked.

"Sure," Courtney said. She got a pen from her backpack. It was a fat pen with six different colors of ink.

Nancy clicked the purple part on top and started to write with purple ink. Then she changed her mind. She clicked the green part. Green ink!

She drew a picture of three large green pizzas.

"How many slices are there in a large pizza?" Nancy asked Bess.

"Eight," Bess said.

"What are you two doing?" George called from across the room.

"Shhh!" Jessie said to George.

George got up and came over to sit with Nancy and Bess.

"What are you doing?" she asked again. But she whispered this time.

"Trying to figure something out," Nancy whispered back. She divided each pizza in her notebook into eight slices.

"How many people live at Laura McCorry's house?" Nancy asked. "Does she have any brothers or sisters?"

"She has a big brother who's in high school," Bess said. "Why?"

"I'm trying to figure out how many slices of pizza Laura's family can eat," Nancy said. "How many do you think her brother would eat?"

"That depends on what kind of pizza it is," George joked.

Nancy laughed, but Bess shook her head.

"No, it doesn't," Bess said. "I've seen her brother. He's huge. He'd eat any kind. I think he'd eat about six slices."

"Okay," Nancy said. She put a *B* for *brother* in six of the slices of pizza in her drawing. "How many do you think Laura's parents would eat?"

"About three each," George said. "So that makes six more."

Nancy wrote a *P* for *parents* in six of the slices.

"I think Laura would eat one or two slices," Bess said.

So Nancy put an *L* for *Laura* in two of the slices. Then she counted up all the slices that were eaten. Fourteen! But that meant ten pieces were still left.

Nancy looked at what she had written in her notebook. Then she reached into the notebook pocket. She took out the notes Rebecca had been sent. She read those again.

"You'll be sorry. Your party is doomed!"

"We have a SECRET."

"We're having a party—and YOU can't come!"

Only the note that had arrived that day was written in blue ink. But the printing was exactly the same as the others.

Nancy squeezed her eyes shut for a minute and asked herself three questions:

1. Who stole the party invitations—and why?

2. Who wrote the notes—and why?

3. Who stole the rose from the top of Rebecca's birthday cake—and why?

Then Nancy opened her eyes. "You know what I think?" she asked.

But Bess and George weren't paying attention to her.

George was watching the movie.

Bess was staring at something behind Nancy. Before Nancy could turn around, Bess opened her mouth as wide as she could and screamed.

Nancy turned around. Framed in the window was a horrible, scary monster with claws!

8

The Secret Comes Out

ancy froze. She stared at the scary face for a minute. It howled and tried to claw the window.

Bess screamed again.

Jessie screamed.

Katie screamed.

Then Rebecca screamed loudest of all. She put her hands to her cheeks and threw her head back. She screamed just like the girl in the haunted house movie.

Only George and Nancy stayed calm.

Nancy went to the front door. Slowly she opened it. George was right behind her.

"Nancy! George! Don't go out there!" the girls cried.

But they didn't listen. Nancy picked up a flashlight that was on a table by the front door. Shining it into the darkness, she walked down the front steps with George and stopped.

Something in the bushes moved.

"Who's there?" Nancy called.

Something in the bushes growled. But it didn't sound like an animal to Nancy. It sounded more like someone she knew.

"No one!" said a boy's voice.

"Come out of there!" George ordered. They waited. Finally the bushes moved again. Someone came out. Another someone followed. It was Jason Hutchings and Mike Minelli.

Jason and Mike were wearing scary makeup. They growled at Nancy and started to run past her.

Just then Mrs. Ramirez came into the yard. She was holding another flashlight.

"What's going on here?" Mrs. Ramirez asked. She shone her light on Jason and Mike. Rebecca and the other girls crowded behind Mrs. Ramirez.

"I told you they were trying to ruin

my party!" Rebecca said. "They stole my party invitations. And wrote those horrible notes. And they took the rose from the cake, too!"

"We didn't do any of that stuff!" Mike Minelli said.

"All we did was squirt you with our water guns," Jason said.

"Huh?" Rebecca said.

"We squirted you when you were outside in the backyard," Mike said. "Jason and David and I sneaked over here and hid behind the bushes. Then we fired our water guns into the air, over the top of the hedge."

"Ohhh!" Bess said. "We thought it was rain."

Jason and Mike laughed.

"That wasn't very nice, boys," Mrs. Ramirez scolded.

The boys tried to stop laughing. But they weren't doing a very good job.

"See?" Rebecca said. "They *were* trying to ruin my party!"

"No, we weren't," Jason said. "We just wanted to have some fun. I had to try out my birthday presents. I got a

water machine gun and this monster
makeup kit."

"But that's all we did," Mike said. "I
promise."

"Liar," Katie said. "Somebody ate the
rose from the cake. It must have been
one of you."

"Never mind, girls," Mrs. Ramirez said.
"Let's go back inside. And, Jason, you
and your friend go back home right now."

Rebecca made a face at Jason. Then,
with her nose in the air, she marched
into the house. Nancy and the other girls
went in, too.

"I don't think he's lying," Nancy said.

"You don't?" George asked. "Why not?"

"Because of the pizza." When Nancy
said this, everyone stopped.

"The pizza?" Rebecca asked.

"Yes." Nancy grinned. "I'll show you.
I think I've figured out the mystery. It's
all in my notebook."

Nancy sat down in the middle of the
sleeping bags. The other girls gathered
around. Even Mrs. Ramirez stood in the
doorway.

"Look at these pizzas," Nancy said,

and she showed them her drawings.

"I can't prove it," Nancy said. "But I think Laura McCorry is having a party right now. That's the secret. There are *three* parties on this block tonight! That's why Laura had so much pizza delivered. She needed extra for her friends."

Rebecca looked from her mother to Nancy. "You think Laura stole my party invitations?"

Nancy nodded. "It would be easy. You said she comes over a lot."

"And you think she sent me those notes?"

Nancy nodded again. "Maybe she has a green pen. But one note was in blue ink. So maybe she has one like this," Nancy said. She held up Courtney's special pen with six colors of ink. "Then she could write in *any* color."

"That *is* Laura's pen!" Courtney said. "I borrowed it from her today at school and forgot to give it back."

"Hmmm," Nancy said. "That must be why the last note was in blue ink. Laura didn't have her pen."

"But what about the rose on the cake?" Bess asked.

"I haven't figured out that part of the mystery yet," Nancy said.

All the girls were very quiet.

"I guess Laura was hurt because I didn't invite her to the party," Rebecca finally said.

"Well, who could blame her?" said Rebecca's mother. "I know I told you that you could only invite eight people. But you played with her all summer. And she does live right across the street."

"What can we do now?" Rebecca asked her mother.

"I'll call Laura's mother," Mrs. Ramirez said. "We'll help you work it out."

A few minutes later the girls heard a knock at the front door. Rebecca ran to open it. Laura, her mother, and two of Laura's friends were standing there. One of them was Lindsay Mitchell. The other was Jennifer Young, another girl from Rebecca's class.

In her hand Laura had a stack of envelopes—the missing party invitations!

"I'm sorry I took these." Laura handed the invitations to Rebecca. "I came over on Tuesday night to borrow your tape player. But you were upstairs. I saw the party invitations on the counter, and there wasn't one for me. I got mad. Anyway, I'm really sorry."

Rebecca looked sad. "Did you write me those notes?" she asked.

Laura nodded.

"Did you steal the biggest rose from the middle of my birthday cake, too?" Rebecca asked.

"No," Lindsay Mitchell said. "I did that. We came over to spy on your party. I saw the cake, and I wanted that rose. I was still mad that I didn't get a cupcake at school. But now I feel bad that I took the rose."

"Well," Rebecca said slowly, "I'm sorry, too. I didn't mean to hurt anyone's feelings."

Rebecca went over to her mother and whispered to her. Mrs. Ramirez nodded, smiled, and gave Laura's mother a wink.

"Laura, will you and Lindsay and Jennifer come to my party now?" Rebecca asked. "My mom said it would be okay. We're watching a scary movie. You could bring your sleeping bags and sleep here."

"Really?" Laura said. She looked at Lindsay and Jennifer. They nodded. "We'll bring the extra pizza, too. We've got tons of it. We ordered too much, even for my brother!"

Everyone laughed. "It's a good thing," Nancy said. "The pizza was my best clue."

"Clue?" Courtney said. "You sound like a detective."

Nancy thought about that. A detective. It sounded good. She would love to solve mysteries when she grew up.

In fact, Nancy thought, she *was* a detective already. She had a special notebook for writing down clues. And she had just solved her first case!

For the next few minutes the girls talked about how Nancy had saved the day. Rebecca passed out the invitations. Everyone loved the hair clips.

Then Mrs. Ramirez told them it was time to settle down. The girls changed into their pajamas and found cozy places to curl up. They started the movie all over again when Laura, Lindsay, and Jennifer returned.

Nancy snuggled into her sleeping bag.

But she wasn't ready to watch the movie yet. She pulled out her notebook. Inside the front cover she wrote:

Nancy Drew's Notebook

Then she turned to the next clean page. It was the one right after the pizza drawings. She wrote:

Today I solved the Case of the Slumber Party Secret. The secret was that you can't keep a party a secret—even if you try.

Rebecca's party turned out okay. She got to give us the invitations she made. They really are neat. So are the rainbow ribbon hair clips. But the best part is that I became a detective.

Next time something mysterious happens, I'll solve that problem, too.

Case closed.